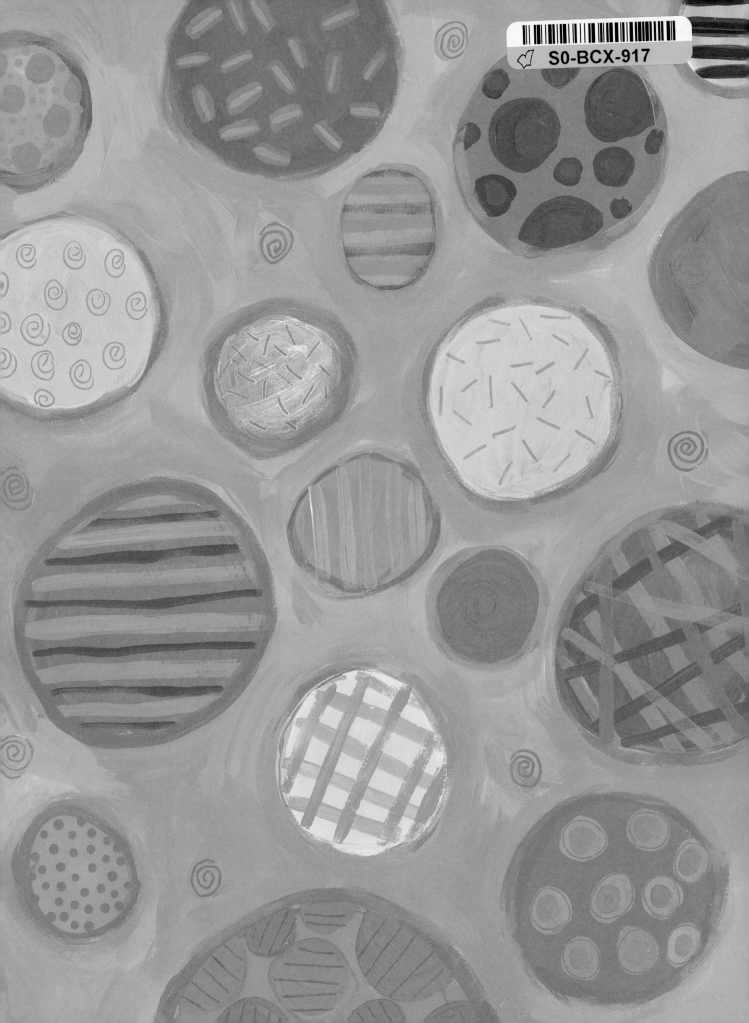

COUNTING COCKATOOS

To Sarah, with much love — Stella Blackstone
To Spencer and Kathleen — Stephanie Bauer

Barefoot Books
124 Walcot Street
Bath, BA1 5BG, UK

Barefoot Books
2067 Massachusetts Ave
Cambridge, MA 02140, USA

Graphic design by Louise Millar, London
Printed and bound in Singapore by Tien Wah Press Ltd
Reproduction by Bright Arts, Singapore

This book was typeset in Providence and Child's Play
The illustrations were prepared in fluid acrylics on 140lb hot press paper

Library of Congress Cataloging-in-Publication Data
Blackstone, Stella.
Counting cockatoos / Stella Blackstone, Stephanie Bauer.
p. cm.
ISBN 1-905236-31-X (hardcover : alk. paper) 1. Counting--Juvenile literature.
2. Animals--Juvenile literature. I. Bauer, Stephanie, ill. II. Title.
QA113.B53 2006
513.2'11--dc22
2005019934

Hardback ISBN 1-905236-31-X

British Cataloguing-in-Publication Data:
a catalogue record for this book
is available from the British Library

1 3 5 7 9 8 6 4 2

counting cockatoos

Written by
stella Blackstone

Illustrated by
stephanie Bauer

Barefoot Books
Celebrating Art and Story

One enormous elephan

and two cockatoos.

2 Two tumbling tigers

and two cockatoos.

3 Three happy hippos

and two cockatoos.

Four rumbling rhinos

and two cockatoos.

5 Five languid lions

and two cockatoos.

6 Six slinking snakes

and two cockatoos.

7 Seven smiling leopard

and two cockatoos.

Eight winking owls

and two cockatoos.

Nine cuddly koalas

and two cockatoos.

10 Ten grinning goldfish

and two cockatoos.

Eleven elegant lizards

and two cockatoos.

12 Twelve toppling turtle

and lots of cockatoos!

From elephants
to cockatoos,
Can you tell me
who is who?

The cockatoos have left behind
some feathers just for you!
Can you count from one to twelve,
and all the feathers, too?

Barefoot Books
Celebrating Art and Story

At Barefoot Books, we celebrate art and story that opens
the hearts and minds of children from all walks of life, inspiring
them to read deeper, search further, and explore their own creative gifts.
Taking our inspiration from many different cultures, we focus on themes that
encourage independence of spirit, enthusiasm for learning, and sharing of
the world's diversity. Interactive, playful and beautiful, our products
combine the best of the present with the best of the past to
educate our children as the caretakers of tomorrow.

www.barefootbooks.com